MOUNTAIN MAN'S LOVE AT FROST SIGHT

SOFIA AVES

First Edition

EBOOK ISBN 978-1-923471-98-6

PRINT ISBN 978-1-923471-20-7

*E*lena Markham never meant to stumble across the bear in the woods. But she did anyway, and then she didn't leave.

Okay, so for a bit she couldn't leave. But let's not go there right now. Let's stick to the story.

It was Christmas. Elena got stuck on a mountain, it snowed, and she stayed with me.

Let's say I convinced her to stay.

Let's say we made friends and had a nice, happy Christmas together.

Yeah, all of this is a huge f*cking lie. Because she didn't stay by choice, and we weren't happy.

At least, not to begin with.

But, she got used to me, and I … grew fond of her.

I'm not good at this lying thing, aren't I?

I'm obsessed with her. In all the best and wrong ways.

So, here's the real story: Elena Markham should never have come to me for help. She should never have told me who hurt her.

And she should never have tried to leave.

*Merry Christmas to me, f*ckers.*

CONTENT WARNING

*G*abe is a sweetie. He's also fairly deranged. His heart is in the right place, at least once you get to know him. It's the getting there part that's interesting. And while we're getting there, we might hit a few triggers. They're below. If you want a nice mountain man read, try RED HART RANCH. It's still suspenseful and a lot of romance and Montana heartstrings, but it's a whole less on the dark side of dark.

IN THIS BOOK you'll find:

- Locking
- Soaking
- Nipple play

- predator/prey
- Dubcon
- Negotiations and deals
- PTSD
- Scarring
- Recounting of assault
- Death
- Abandonment
- Comfort eating
- Knife violence
- Deboning
- Stretching
- Fisting

PLEASE READ SAFELY. Mountain Men (especially Gabe) aren't made for real world situations. But they do make excellent book boyfriends.

IF YOU DON'T HAVE one, I'll lend you mine.

SOFIA xx

For all the locked doors that should stay locked.
Sometimes they get opened.

PROLOGUE

A pretty girl comes up my mountain and I fall in love. That's how this love at first sight thing works, right? Let's pretend she's more than pretty. Beautiful, actually. Strawberry blonde hair that tumbles over her shoulders in glorious waves that a man can wrap his hands around his fists and the sort of hips that rough, calloused fingers can sink into without hurting her. Let's pretend she's stunning.

Actually, let's not pretend at all.

Her name is Elena Markham, and three days before Christmas, she walked up my mountain, the one a few behind Hope Peak, and asked for my help.

I promised her I'd give it and she stayed.

We've been happy ever since.

Now, what if I said that my favorite game is two truths and a lie? Can you pick out the parts that's bullshit in that little segue of my antisocial life? Because that last part *is* true. I don't go into town more often than I need to—which is about three times a year, and only for the sorts of supplies I can't garner out here for myself.

And I sure as hell don't need other people around me.

Let me give you a hint: Elena Markham came to me. She asked for help.

And those hips of hers are made for fucking.

How much of the rest is bullshit, I'll let you decide for yourself.

CHAPTER ONE

GABE

$\mathcal{I}$ haven't dealt with a single person in over four months, and that's the way I like it.

Hope Peak is the sort of small town in Montana that you can pass through on a tourist drive or stop and stay for a lifetime. It's the sort of small town that has secrets, a rumor mill that rivals any government agency in its efficiency, and a population so inbred that it keeps men like me away for most of the year.

I lie. There are no other men like me around my part of the town. Or more accurately, the part of the town that I'm farthest from.

Years ago, I took the advice of a ranger in that same town after I came back from a desert mission and hiked into the mountains. After a week of messing around, I came back into town, found the land owner I needed to speak to and paid double what the little slice of peace that I found for myself was worth in order to keep the rest of the world at bay.

Which is why, when I stare through my rifle's scope and see the sort of mark that has nothing to do with my dinner but has the potential to sate a very different sort of appetite altogether, my interest sparks.

The woman in my mountains has no right to be here, and that makes her all the more fascinating.

Dressed in a dark green jacket that covers her to the knees but hangs open with a fluffy hood, I think she's a damn bear at first and nearly end her life before I have a chance to find out anything about her. But she's not a bear, or even a small bear, at that. The moment the flash of red of her checkered shirt, knotted at her navel to expose the swell of her stomach catches my eye, my focus shifts significantly. From there she's all curves of the luxurious sort. Not the hiker sort, that's for fucking sure. The sort a man can sink his hands into and—well. Do some damage. Her pale, tight jeans look painted on, and a fantasy of peeling them from her to find out how her flesh dimples beneath my roughened hands infiltrates my mind within seconds.

Hell, I'm an ex-soldier not a saint, for fuck's sake. And I never did get myself a Christmas present this season, Here's one ready made to order just for me.

Strawberry blonde hair is wound into a messy knot on top of her head, though plenty of strands escape around her face. Dirt streaks one cheek where it looks like she's battled a trash panda. Her rose stained lips are turned up in a pensive smile that reflects inward as she climbs the last boulder to reach my yard.

That boulder that may as well have a *keep out* sign attached to it for its aggressive profile.

At least she's wearing sturdy boots as she traverses the thin trail that leads toward my cabin after she climbs as though that's her only destination with a few days to go until Christmas. But it's the quick glance as she checks over her shoulder like she expects there to be traffic on this deserted road of mine and the haunted look in her pretty, sky blue eyes when she turns back my way that grips me at stomach level and refuses to let go.

Christ. What sort of bait is she that she's out here alone and fucking miles from anywhere?

Answer: the sort that I want to take hold of and find out what the hell she's doing here and why she's on my land.

Which means it's time to show my hand.

Lowering my rifle a fraction, I step away from

the hide I've been resting behind and let her see me. She freezes, widening those pretty eyes framed with thick lashes. Her hands splay at her sides. Breaths come short before they stall altogether. I can almost taste her panic, relish the way she wants to bolt, because I'll chase her down and we both know it.

She won't make it as far as the Red Cedar that's just beyond my place before I take her to the ground beneath me and start my interrogation. The thought of finding out what those curves feel like first hand against my skin is enough to send blood roaring south a second time.

"Here, kitty, kitty," I murmur, just to antagonize the shit out of her as I lower my rifle a little more.

Enough to give myself freedom to chase her when she runs.

Enough to let her think she has a chance if she does.

Her feet angle towards my cabin like she thinks she might beat me there and lock me out. It's cute, the tiniest signs of hope she displays.

"You live here?" she calls, her voice loud enough to bounce off the granite rocks around me.

Defiant and sassy as all hell.

I love her attitude. This is going to be fun.

"This is private property." I suppose I'm supposed to put on a show of humanity or some other bullshit around what's probably a local girl or some tourist out to climb the mountains.

In winter. With snow coming on that's been holding off for a week or more this season already.

Christ. She must have a death wish.

Where the hell is her pack?

"People don't usually come out here."

There's a reason I'm out this far on my own, honey. A man like me isn't fit for human consumption.

Especially not for a woman like you.

She might have figured that out on her own by now. Not that it seems to deter her.

"People might not, but I do. I'm looking for someone."

I quirk an eyebrow. "Not anyone else is out here to be found."

"Who says I'm looking for anyone else?" The sassy tone is back in her voice.

That sass calls to me like honey.

I'm so fucked just looking at her that it takes a moment too long for her words to register. "Why are you out here?" My rifle rises. I relax my grip with effort.

That rifle has been an extension of my arm for decades. It kept me safe in deserts that contain sand that's a different color to this country. Shit, I can still taste that pink dust on the back of my tongue on nights when it's snowing outside and too damn damp for grit to be fucking anywhere. But it's damn well there anyway.

That rifle stayed with me all the way home. I

nursed it on my lap right next to the box that held my best friend. The only time I put it down was to kneel before his mother and beg her forgiveness.

Then I brought my ass up north and walked away from the rest of the world.

I've been here ever since, and that rifle has saved my life countless times. Kept me fed, too. Now, that same rifle feels heavy in my grip. For the first time, I wonder if I've been holding on to it too tightly.

"Who are you looking for, honey?" I ask softly.

Too softly.

Her chin rises.

She's all sass and filthy from her walk up my mountain. Dirty in all the right sort of ways. When she pops a hip with the sort of smile that promises sin, my blood runs hot despite my inner reflections.

The effects this woman has on me, when I don't even know her name, is insanity itself.

"You're Gabriel Decker, right?" She watches me carefully.

I nod slowly. She knows my name. That's...something new. A game changer for sure. I keep my grip on my rifle all the same.

"That's right." *Just because you know who I am doesn't stop me from wanting to play, honey.*

"Good." Her feet plant firmly in the hard packed dirt before me. "Because I'm sick of walking. I need your help."

I huff a laugh under my breath. Who in the hell

has this woman been talking to in Hope Peak that gave her the impression that I'm one of the good guys? Because I'm sure as hell not one. She can keep thinking that if she likes. It'll mean a cute surprise for both of us.

Merry fucking Christmas to me.

CHAPTER TWO

ELENA

*G*abriel Decker looks exactly the way I was told to expect him to appear: the epitome of mountain man rugged kitsch. Not that I expect he'll self-diagnose any of that from the expression on his weathered face, or the little I can see of it around his wild beard. Beneath the unmanicured bush his lip curls in what might be a sneer or a smile. I know it's going to take me a while to interpret some of his expressions.

A black Henley is worn beneath a tan jacket that shows signs of wear over khaki pants. Boots that look as sturdy as the mountain he stands on are on his feet. Hair covers his head and face in a wild tangle that leaves me itching to comb my fingers through it and discover the man beneath.

But I don't need to do any of that. Because his eyes—grey laced with shots of green like he's been carved from the side of the mountain itself—stare back at me. Or through me, as though he can possess me with a single stare.

Good. Because I hauled my not inconsiderable ass all the way up into his mountain range today for a reason.

Not because I'm a princess, but because of…preferences. One of which may have followed me up the mountain, which is why I spent half a day scrambling through underbrush and hoping that the only bear I come across in his mountains is the one that I'm looking for.

Before him, I feel small.

Gabriel stares at me like he thinks I'm looking for something that's not here. But I'm not searching for the good guy. Gabriel Decker isn't a hero—at least, not any more from what I've heard—and he's not what I need right now.

But I do need the skills he offers, and I'm willing to pay for that service.

The man I climbed a mountain for steps closer. His hold on the oversized gun that matches his size never wavers.

Good.

"If you know my name, and you don't expect

anyone else to be out here..." He pauses and holds my gaze with those strange mountain god eyes that suck me right in. "Do you mind telling me why you keep looking over my shoulder like you keep expecting extra company when you don't have an invitation to be here?"

The faintest smile tugs at my lips. I like a man who gets right to business. Actually, I've always preferred the company of men to women, and with six brothers that's been my natural habitat for a long time. At least, it used to be. My smile fades.

"I have a business proposition for you."

He leans against the next boulder. Not the one he emerged from behind, but the one closest to me. "You do, huh? Wanna come inside and talk this through, *Miss I-climbed-a mountain-to-find-you-and-you-already-know-my name-but-I-don't-have-any-idea-who-the-fuck-you-are?*" His genial tone erodes as he talks, like the sun disappearing behind a cloud. He shifts away from his boulder, stalking forward until he stops right in front of me. A wall of pure muscle wrapped up in a Henley and other soft materials.

I doubt I'll find anything so gentle underneath.

Hard ass. I knew he would be, a man with his history. He brought back his best friend from an overseas hell where they were both kept prisoners, only they were never let go and only one of them escaped. He was able to bring his best friend home because he couldn't stand leaving him there.

That's the man I need now.

Going inside with him is a really stupid move. It's also where I need to be right now, to break this impasse.

"Sure." I put on the flirtatious persona he seems to love so much even though my energy is fading fast after my day long hike. "Got enough coffee in there to pep a girl up?"

Gabriel Decker stares me down for a long moment before he pivots ninety degrees and walks around me like I'm an object he has to avoid. Like we're magnets that repel each other if we get too close.

But that's a lie. Because I read the heat in his eyes when I first stumbled out of the forest and into the clearing, back when he dropped his scope and looked at me. Really looked at me. A rawness was written there and it had less to do with lust and more to do with a vulnerability that I'm not sure the mountain man before me knows about himself.

This will be a fun visit.

I follow him and hope I don't have to chip stale coffee out of a tin in order to stave off a fast growing caffeine headache. Perhaps I should have brought my own emergency sachets in order to combat a situation just like this one.

A girl can't be too careful, after all. And I need my coffee to function.

"Lead the way," I murmured to his back.

A falter in Gabriel's step is the only indication he hears my attitude. Brief and short, and quickly rectified, but it's there. He takes strides much longer than I can naturally keep up with to get to the cabin door. The rest of the building seems to disappear into the thick tree line behind the house as though, like him, it has emerged from the forest by some magical accident and shouldn't be here.

Yep, I definitely came to the right man to fix my little problem.

I swivel back to check the clearing around the cabin but all that's there are the tools of a workman: a half cut log pile; a fire pit area that's seen recent use and has been swept clean. Lanterns hang at intervals on trees that I walked through, hidden in the boughs. Each is attached by an electrical cord that has to be solar powered all the way out here. For a man who is dead set on zero visitors, Decker sure knows how to create a mood, and I haven't even seen the place lit up yet.

But I can sure imagine how pretty this place must look after dark.

Not a single cobweb is in sight. The cabin and its surroundings are cleaner than most suburban homes. I wrap my arms around myself, ignoring the ache in my chest.

"I've got coffee. It's not half as shit as you imagine. None of it is." Gabriel's voice softens a fraction on that last part.

I turn my attention back to him. "Thank you." My voice catches.

"I wouldn't use those words with me, honey." His hand flexes on the heavy door with its many locks.

I study them and close the distance into his space, taking in the size difference between us in full. Out of the sunlight, beneath the oversized eaves of the cabin that match him, the difference is—

Well, huge. Like him. He stands a least one and a half times taller, dwarfing me. I shiver as I run my hands over the shiny locks that look as though they're serviced regularly.

"Are bears good at working keys out here?" I mutter, tracing the locks with my fingertips.

"I told you I don't do visitors." His short answer makes sense.

The locks don't.

I nod anyway. "You mentioned coffee."

"So I did." He jerks his head sideways, gesturing for me to head inside. "Follow the hallway and head upstairs." His lips quirk beneath his beard. "I'll lock up."

"You… Upstairs?" I blink.

"Follow the hallway, honey. There's only one way to go." He leans into my space, pressing a large hand to my lower back and gives me a little push. "In you go."

Warm spreads across my back followed by tiny shocks. I trip over the threshold to the music of his laughter, and stumble into the dimness beyond. The door closes as he mutters to himself.

I reach for a wall, finding one. That gives me relief as I wander along the hallway, my eyes adjusting to the odd light just as my feet find the first step.

And my mind begs the question: if the locks aren't for keeping bears out, who or what are they keeping *in*?

Refusing to give grace to the panic brewing in my gut and the fear that the monster I've left outside is lesser than the one at my back, I climb the stairs. Coffee will fix everything.

And it had better be damned good, as promised.

CHAPTER THREE

ELENA

*M*y legs hate me. That's the only message that gets to my brain as I climb the stairs that seem to go on forever. My hand trails the smooth banister that winds through what feels like the inside of a huge tree trunk—for all I know, that's exactly what it is. Why shouldn't my mountain man also double it down as a tree god in his spare time? And then I see the light at the top of the stairwell. It's a literal hallelujah moment. I could cry.

Actually, I could probably crawl.

My knees wobble as I lean forward, reaching for the glowy part that looks like opening at the end of the stairs. I really am ready to drop and haul my body up step by step. What I told Gabriel earlier—that I was sick of walking and ready to stay forever—wasn't exactly a lie. I do need to plant my butt and hiking was not my favorite thing. My body is *not* made for exercise of any type. Okay, maybe one thing. But that's about it.

"Not just yet. You can make it, honey." Gabriel's deep tones wrap around me along with his hands as he physically hauls me up the next step and the next. "Six more to go."

"It feels like an eternity," I grumble. "Why can't you stay on the ground like everyone else?"

"You'll see." He squeezes my waist, heavy, his thick fingers sinking into my flesh.

I bite back the moan that threatens when one finger slides over my hip bone and hits that freaking sensitive spot that leaves me all shivery and loose boned. The mountain man behind me huffs. Damnit, he knows *exactly* what he's doing.

Drake warned me about this man.

Yeah, and I ignored those warnings because I need what Gabriel Decker offers.

"Don't do that," I mutter, because getting a breath in when he's doing that and being near this man is damn near impossible.

"Help you, honey?" The laughter in his voice is barely constrained.

"You know what," I mutter, slapping at his hands like his touch is offensive.

Spoilers: his touch is so far from offensive that I'm trembling all over, and we can both feel that.

He doesn't stop his version of helping me, and he doesn't let go.

"Three more," he says quietly. "You can make it, honey."

"Elena," I pant, and not from exertion. "My name is Elena Markham."

"Mmm." he makes a low noise in his chest that might be approval at my giving him my name, or not. "Well, Elena Markham, welcome to my home. Sorry it's not to your...liking." He lifts me the last few steps and deposits me on the smooth, hard wood floor that forms an open canopy above the forest.

This is why my legs hurt. This is why they shake so badly.

We're at tree height of the giant kind. Above the canopy, almost.

I can see the nearest neighbors, and we're at the same level. And I can see them because...there are no walls. Well, one, if it counts. Behind me. The rest of the house is... open.

Gabriel Decker's mountain home is one giant tree house complete with a huge lily pad style arched roof that looks straight out into more mountains than I have ever seen in my life.

I stare and stare with my mouth open. I think a little drool comes out. A gentle hand closes my mouth. Gentle fingers stroke my jawline in a featherlight touch, so at odds with the bulk of the huge, rough-hewn man drawn from the side of the mountain that instead of staring at the vista laid out before me, I'm staring at him instead.

"Breathe, Elena," he murmurs.

Hearing my name on his lips for the first time does strange things to my brain. I barely respond as he settles beside me on the floor, ignoring the wooden, hand carved furniture scattered about the enormous platform like room.

His shoulder nudges mine as he turns away to look out at the mountains beyond his, his jaw set in a determined line, the diamond hard quality visible even beneath the scruff of his beard.

Once more the desire to run my fingers through the mass of curly fibers slams into me. I knot my hands in my lap and press downward to prevent any unintentional groping.

"You said you need my help."

Ah, negotiations have started. I didn't expect him to do small talk but he really has gotten right down to it.

"You said you have coffee," I counter.

"I do." He turns his head to look at me, his arms slung loosely over his knees.

The sheer presence of this enormous man hits me again. I tuck my knees beneath me, squeezing my fingers together. *Looks like that coffee isn't coming any time soon.* A shuddering breath releases from my chest.

"You were a sniper, right?" I check, but he doesn't seem to have brought his rifle up to the platform living area with him. *Did you lock up below? I pray you did.*

That conversation with Drake back at Hope Peak in Perfect Brews runs through my mind at double the speed it actually happened.

"What sort of help do you need, Elena?"

"The sort that will end a problem forever."

Drake's sigh as he looked me over hit me bone deep. It was a judgey sigh and I wanted to slap it out of him. "You've been like a sister to me since college, Lena. I hate seeing you like this."

"Like what?"

"Doubting yourself. Fearing every shadow."

I pressed a hand to my stomach over my shirt. "Shadows have claws."

Drake nodded, sipped his beer. "Then I know a man. Someone you can trust in this."

"Good. I can pay." I had plenty of money. My career had seen to that.

Drake's pensive assessment never faded as he watched me over the rim of his schooner. "Elena. Trust him to get the job done. But don't turn your back to him. Not for one second. There's a reason life made him the man he is."

A week after that conversation with my oldest friend, one who still talks to me, I sit in Gabriel

Decker's house, a damn long way from anywhere. I'm begging a cup of coffee from him, and about to tell him why I'm here. Somehow, I suspect he's as dangerous as Drake suggested.

And the one time my back was to him, he helped me. Touched me. I reacted to him in a way I've never reacted to a man before.

What does that say about him? About me?

The locks on his door remind me of Drake's words. A shiver riots over my body.

"Cold?" Gabriel murmurs.

"Uncertain." What is it about him that's like a truth bomb in action? I can't lie no matter how much I try.

"Fair enough." He nods at my side, never looking my way.

I decide to go with the flow and keep blurting out the hardest truth that I couldn't say when I was seated across from Drake that day in Hope Peak. Perfect Brews isn't exactly the best place for quiet conversation if you want what's said to go unheard.

"My ex is trying to kill me."

The moment the words leave my mouth I regret them. They hang in the air of Gabriel's stunning home, shattering the sense of serenity he's garnered in this quiet space away from everything and everyone out here. I've brought my sense of unmuted chaos here into his home, and I have no right to do that. No matter what scars this silent man beside me carries—and I'm sure there are many —he doesn't deserve to be dragged into the bullshit I've brought onto myself.

I shake my head, pushing up on screaming thighs that can't deal with a yoga class let alone a hike then the world's biggest stair climber activity. "I shouldn't have come here. This is wrong."

The hand that wraps around my wrist closes like a manacle. Forest green and granite eyes meet mine, barely constrained fury blazing behind them.

"You came up my mountain seeking something, Elena Markham. You'll stay until you get it."

Shit, shit, shit. This is the part people don't tell you about the bear in the woods theory.

Sometimes the bear is a little protective. Sometimes they're a little mad. And something in me wants all that.

So, so badly.

But also, I'm scared that what I want might clash with what I've come to find. And that's so much more critical that any want on my tick sheet from here on in.

But from the way that the mountain man holds onto my wrist and refuses to let go, there's a different sort of trouble brewing.

CHAPTER FOUR

GABE

"*L*et go," Elena murmurs, staring up at me with dilated eyes. "Please."

She doesn't pull away, and she doesn't flinch. Not once.

I already have a damn good idea of why she's in my home and who sent her my way. The fact that she's likely come from a domestic abuse situation—assuming I've guessed correctly from the little she's already said—and hasn't run screaming from me yet is telling.

But then, she knew who I was before she walked up my mountain. Or at least, she thought she did.

I loosen my hold on her wrist, enough to let her

turn her hand in my grip, but not free herself. "Tell me about him."

"Coffee. Please?" The fragment of hope in her eyes is so fucking sweet that I almost cave and give her what she wants.

Almost.

"Soon, sweetness." I rub the pad of my thumb across her wrist, pleased when her pulse flutters erratically beneath my touch. "What do I need to know about him?"

The light fades from her pretty gaze. "You're no fun," she grumbles. That's cute, too.

"Talk now. Reward later."

"Hmmph." She glances up at me through her lashes and flexes her hand in my grasp, uncurling her fingers like she's tickling salmon.

Is the little toy fucking flirting with me?

I swallow hard and tug her across the floor toward me. The patch we're on is worn smooth from years of me walking on it.

"Tell me about him, Elena." I let an edge of hardness enter my tone, squeezing her wrist a little firmer.

Her pulse quickens. "His name is Oliver. Oliver Markham." Her chin rises, the same show of defiance she gave me back in the yard.

"You kept his name?" That's something. If she's divorced, he's fair game. If she's not... He's still in a world of hurt if he's damaged the stunning woman before me and stole the light from her.

"The paperwork hasn't come through yet. For the name change," she adds quickly at my assessing look. "Everything else is finalized. Not that he didn't fight. He's a bit obsessive." She looks down at where I still hold her wrist. Her hand goes limp.

My heart aches in my chest. "Show me, sweetness."

Her gaze shoots to meet mine. For the first time since she arrived on my land, there's real fear in her eyes. "What?"

"Show me what he did to you."

"I told you."

I smile, and there's no humor in it. "You gave me words, Elena. Now I want you to show me what he did to you to make you want to leave." I release her wrist, the hardest damn thing I've done in an age, and give her space.

For a woman I met less than an hour ago and just brought it to my house, that's saying something.

She wraps her arms around herself like a protective barrier, staring up at me. Those pretty lips move, but nothing comes out. For the longest time I'm sure I'll be responsible for resuscitating her with coffee just for being an asshole. Then she shifts again, and I realize that the single person hug hasn't been about hiding from me. It's been about motivating herself to do exactly what I asked.

35

Her hands fall to her sides, along with the panels of her red checkered shirt. The material hangs open in the middle, displaying the same slice of deliciously curved stomach she showed me before, along with a fresh patch of skin. But this flesh is neither soft nor unmarked.

It's crisscrossed with deep scars, and not the sort she might have done herself in the middle of an anxiety attack or worse.

The edges are jagged, like the blade he used was serrated. A hunting or fishing knife is my guess. He didn't go too deep, but whether that was by design or choice is anyone's guess.

"Christ, sweetness," I murmur. "You think he followed you out here?"

I hope he's followed her. I hope he's stupid enough to try to break into my home. That'll give me a damned good reason to end the threat to her life in short order. I can be as creative as she needs me to be about body disposal.

"I– I'm not sure." The words expel from her in a rush. She knots her fingers but doesn't try to hide her body from my gaze. "I might just be paranoid."

Again, that flicker of defiance hits me low in my gut. I'm blown away by the display of courage before me from a woman who knows fuck all about me. What she does has been garnered from a stranger.

"Being paranoid might keep you alive." I rise to my feet and hold out my hand. She hesitates then pushes up. Her legs wobble but she refuses my help, the strain in her face obvious. Pain lances through her eyes as she looks away from me.

I grab the edges of her shirt and start buttoning it up. She gives a little gasp and pulls back for the first time.

Elena's hands rise to bat at mine. "If you want me to cover up—"

I let out a soft growl that stops her fussing. "I do, but not for the reasons you're thinking. Is he armed?"

"What?" She stands still and lets me button her shirt to her breasts. My knuckles graze the heavy swell, and her eyelids half close. "Y-yes. Knives. He prefers knives."

I can see that, honey. "I can deal with hand-to-hand. Is he trained?"

"Not like you."

That gives me pause. She asked about my work before. "What do you know about me?" I let my hands linger on that top button of her top. My thumbs stroke the curves of her breasts.

Her breaths come a little faster. "Only that you've been out here for a long time. You came home after— After your world was destroyed." Her voice becomes a thin whisper as I drop one hand to her hip and press her backwards into the door to the stairwell I closed and locked earlier.

"Good. Keep going." I squeeze her hip, reaching up to cup her jaw. "What else did he tell you?"

"Who?" Her eyes glaze as I close my hand around her throat gently. Not threatening, just there.

"Drake." I stroke her pulse point there, too.

"He said not to..." Her eyes flutter open. She's struggling, fighting me, and it's beautiful. "He said not to... That there's a reason you are the way you are."

He got that damn right.

"Drake should keep his opinions to his own damn self," I mutter, pulling my hand away from her hip to brace my forearm over her head, boxing her against the door to my open air living space. "So tell me, Elena with the husband you're asking me to kill. What are you offering in payment?"

Her eyes refocus and she looks out over my shoulders. "How do you keep all the nasties out?" she mutters.

I laugh, a sound alien to me. "Damn, woman. You're gonna make me crazier than I already am." I stoke her throat and she fucking well arches in my hold like a cat being petted. If I wasn't hard before, now I'm straining in my jeans and fit to burst from that little display. Touching her was the worst choice of my day. "Focus, sweetness. Is he down there now, looking for you, or are you just scared of him?"

She shakes her head, restless. "I'm fucking terri-fied, alright? He cut me up, chased me across three counties. I managed to get a divorce only because he didn't realize that I'd spent the past decade building my own business while he was off screwing anything with tits on business flights. I was meant to be the pretty southern wife who could cook and raise kids." A bitter smile twists her pretty lips. "Only, if he'd ever actually listened during any of the dates we had during those early days, he would have realized that I struggled to fall pregnant or keep a baby, because there's something wrong with me. And after he fucked me up…well. He made that a permanent thing, didn't he?"

I swallow hard as her eyes glitter with the sort of madness that I know all too well. It's the same sort I'll see if I look in a mirror. Not that I've seen one of those for a damn long time.

"Did he?" I let her throat go and cup her cheek. "I'll do what you want, honey. Maybe throw in a few extra details if you need me to be specific."

I want to see if she's got desperation on her mind, or revenge. Not that I much care. I'll do what she wants anyway. Right now we're just negotiating terms. The man's life became forfeit the moment she showed me her scars.

"I don't care what you do. As long as he's gone." Her eyes fill with tears, but they aren't for the dead man to be. They're for the woman she was who trusted him with something that was precious to her once.

"I'll do that for you," I say softly. "You mentioned payment, Elena. What do you have in mind?"

"I have money," she blurts, then winces, like it's a dirty word.

Between us it is, and she instinctively knows that.

I laugh at her. I don't need a dead man's money.

"What the hell am I going to do with cash, sweetness? I've got more than I need and nothing to spend it on. I got a payout enough to last me four lifetimes when I retired and walked out here. Hell, they gave me three medals for what I did. And what I didn't do." My voice becomes ragged.

"I heard." Her fingers rise to my shoulder. It's about as far as she can reach without getting onto her toes. "How do you know Drake?"

I frown at her. "He served with me for a few years. But he's not a stranger to you, is he?" I got that wrong. Maybe I've assumed other things about her, too.

She shakes her head, her eyes clearing. "We went to college together. He did engineering. I studied music. Then I graduated and grew up. My love became a hobby...forgotten." Her lips twist again. "And I got a new hobby."

I fucking hate that expression on her.

"The husband." I brush my thumb across her bottom lip, smoothing her flesh out. Her skin pops back under my touch. "Alright, honey. The deal is that you stay here, and you don't leave. That's it.

That's my payment. Stay out of my way. I'll tell you when the job is done. You'll be free of him then. Understood?" I drop my hands and step back. If I don't, the job won't get done, but she sure as hell will.

Elena nibbles her lip. "Drake said…"

I raise both eyebrows. "Drake should keep his opinions to himself. The kitchen is around the back." I wave a hand to the hollowed section behind where she stands. It's bigger than it looks from here, but she'll find that out in a moment. "The doors stay locked. Both of them. Everything you need is up here. Explore. Do *not* leave." I fix her with a hard stare. "If you do, I'll find you. That won't be pretty, sweetness. Coffee is behind you. Twenty steps or less. Make as much mess as you like. The place is yours."

I wait for her tentative nod, then step back in measured paces. I don't count the steps out in my head. I don't need to.

I built the house years ago, and I know the dimensions of every single piece of hewn wood in my home. I keep walking as she watches my retreat, frowning. Know the moment that her mouth opens that I'm close. I reach overhead and grab the harness, linking it to my waist. My rifle—my other rifle, not the one I stowed away in the locker downstairs—is at the edge. I grab it a fraction of a second before the freefall takes me.

Her cry is the prettiest thing I've heard in a long damn time.

I wonder if she'll do that for me when I slide inside her after I've killed the man who marked her up and tried to steal the defiance from her.

The man who failed.

I won't.

My name echoes off the mountains as I taste her panic and disbelief in a single breath in the moment before my feet hit the ground. I unclip the harness and stow it safely in its place until I return for her.

Stay there, sweetness. Don't you dare leave.

Elena peers down at me, her hands gripping the edge. Her mouth frames my name in a silent cry.

You'll say it louder later, beautiful.

I promise.

I shoulder my rifle, its weight a comfort as I walk away from her, knowing it might be a while before I return.

Hopefully the ex is a better stalker than she thinks. Hopefully he's a mean piece of work.

I look forward to finding out what his fear tastes like before I go home and make his wife mine.

CHAPTER FIVE

ELENA

I've wondered for three days who is dead: Oliver or Gabriel.

For three days, I've wondered why I care. And so for three days, I've cooked.

Gabriel's treehouse is anything but rustic. I crawled to the edge of the platform when he left and stared down at him in the sling, sailing away from me.

Don't leave. Understand?

Leaving me in a place where I had no idea where anything was, how anything worked, or when or if he would return.

Because I hadn't told him everything about Oliver. I hadn't told him about the endless resources at his disposal. The amount of security that surrounds him at all times.

Gabriel never gave me a chance to explain.

Or maybe I never offered.

He left, I screamed. I cried. I made myself coffee.

I explored. I cooked.

The whole treehouse concept seems to work on solar panels. I had no idea how many or where, but they are enough to power my energy consumption and manic food efforts. And the man has a pantry to match my needs. A kitchen stocked with everything I required.

And a bookshelf and bathroom beneath the stars to match.

It was like this man has been custom made to match me, and now he's gone. I've sent him to what is probably his death and to get out of the treehouse, I'll either have to learn to pick a lock or jump.

The only thing Gabriel's house doesn't come with is connectivity. Naturally. Why would he need a phone? Or the internet? Or satellite? I suppose that last is pushing it. He has everything else, and enough coffee to outlast even a caffeine addict like me.

When night set in on that first evening, I sat in the far corner of his bed in a pillow fort designed to keep the world out and waited for something to come and eat me.

But.. nothing did.

Nary a squirrel, wild cat, or bug flew into the

space. I have no idea if my mountain man rubbed some sort of oil into the wooden arches or had trained the local wildlife to stay away—I wouldn't put anything past him at this point. I still can't force myself to lie down. So I stare at that spot where he walked backwards off the platform like he might pop back up for no reason at all. Like he might just return with an easy *"honey, I'm home,"* and we can play happy families.

But we aren't, of course.

Don't leave.

I have no future, and Oliver Markham drove away my past. None of my family speak to me anymore, not even my brothers, not after the way he treated them for the past years. Not that I blame them. They tried, but toxic is toxic and Oliver wears the crown.

I pray that Gabriel finds it and chokes him with it.

Now I sit on the bed that's not as terrifying, staring into the darkness that's not as cloying and thick as it was on that first night. It's an odd feeling to put all my trust and belief into a stranger that I met a few days ago. Someone I didn't know existed and who didn't know my name, but who heroes me anyway.

What will you give me as payment?

Don't leave.

I tried. For those first two days I tried so hard. I

worked those locks just like I think he expected. I kicked the door and a few other things. I considered trying to slide down the rope even or pulling it back up but he'd done something at his end that made both those actions a one way suicide journey.

I'm not in that much of a hurry to die.

I know what he wants. And the worst part is that even with the conditions that he's given me, my body refuses to rebel. My mind either.

If he doesn't return, Oliver wins. I'll be sitting here, eating the cakes and sweets I've baked until he finds me and ends it anyway. I can't fight him anymore. It's been years and I've run out of anger for him.

All that's left is fear.

If Gabriel does what he's promised then I can feed him before he collects his...payment.

I swallow hard at the prospect. It's not that Gabriel isn't a beautiful man. He is, in a rugged, damaged way. Like me, only more striking. Wild. There's a sense of procession about him so different to Oliver. My ex wanted a tool. Something he could call on to do a job and nothing more.

Stand here. Do this. Look pretty. Pose and smile.

Now go back in your box and wind down until I need you again, little toy.

Life with Oliver was like a hellish ballet where I was a backup dancer in my own life.

Something tells me that Gabriel's version of

possession will be a different beast, and I'm here for it. You'd think I'd be sick of being treated that way by a man by now, but I've never reacted to anyone the way I did when he touched me. I *trust him* and that's beyond huge for me. That I didn't want him to leave me alone screamed something to me and I've spent the last days deciphering that, and how I feel.

That I want him to come back.

Maybe I want to stay, with some conditions.

Maybe.

Or maybe I want to run. Or fly like he did off the edge.

Or maybe I have no idea what's going on in my own head. I need to sleep properly tonight and not watch the forest close in around me.

It should be freezing up here, but it's not. There are furnaces built in on one side, and the quilts on his oversized bed are ridiculously warm. I make a marshmallow of them with me in the middle. It's like being in the center of a burrito. When I doze, I topple sideways and as the night darkens, splayed across the bed that's four times too big for a woman my size.

I dream of gazelles chasing lions across mountain ranges and salmon drowning bears in rivers that flow in the wrong direction upstream. A harsh noise like a chainsaw interrupts my sleep. I've never been a lucid dreamer, but even I know that noise isn't supposed to be there. I flap a hand but mine are pressed tight to my sides. The bear and the salmon are close. Too close. Water and breath mingle, and one of them can't breathe. I forget which one I am in the dream sequence as I try to flail about in the over-sized bed and fail.

"Elena. Jesus– What the fuck? Girl. You need help." An amused voice pierces my dream, bringing me up a level.

I can breathe. I gasp about like a guppy drowning in an excess of fresh air. "Stuck," I croak. "Salmon don't talk."

"Fucked if I know what salmon do, sweetness, but you've done a damn fine job of knotting yourself in here." Large hands glide along my sides and extract me from the bear's furry grip.

Or maybe it's the bear who saves me.

My dream sequence is all out of whack as I pry my eyes open and try to unravel the reality before me.

"Gabriel?"

"You ruined my bed, sweetness." The hands wrapped around me squeeze gently. He seems to have a thing about that. Dark eyes survey me as I piece together the face before me and come up with one I recognize in the darkness. "What are you wearing?"

"Your shirt." It's still night. The plethora of stars I've spent nights studying are studded against midnight velvet, crisp and clear. Now that I'm out of my marshmallow cocoon, my skin and the night air clash. A shiver rips through me. "Cold," I mutter, knotting my legs up and my arms around myself. The hem of his shirt tugs to the tops of my thighs.

Gabriel's eyes track the movement. "It looks good on you."

"The cold?"

"My shirt." His fingertips trace the edge of the material next to my thighs, starting from the outside and work their way in.

Suddenly I'm not cold at all.

"You were away for three days," I whisper.

His fingers trace inward and halt at the join of my legs. He pauses, his breaths long and even. "I did what you asked," he says eventually.

My heart pounds in my chest. "He's gone?"

Darkness obscures Gabriel Decker's eyes. He doesn't nod or make any other confirming movement. "Yes."

I shiver. My reaction has nothing to do with the outside conditions inside Gabriel's house.

"That's what you wanted isn't it, Elena?"

I hold his gaze. "Yes."

He nods. "Good." Those fingers press between my legs. "Open."

I let out a shuddering breath. "I'm not—"

"You're exactly what I want," He cuts me off. "We agreed on the terms before I left. I told you not to leave. The job is done, and here you are.'" With every word he arches his body over mine a fraction, his hand pressing downward all the time, spreading my legs open as he demanded. "Is there something I missed, *sweetness?*"

I fist a hand to his shoulder, barely able to breathe. "I– I'm not ready for this," I confess, letting him spread me wide. The shirt that I stole hitches around my waist, not covering my lower half at all. I know the moment his hand presses between my legs he'll find me drenched. The betrayal I can't prevent. My cheeks heat as I stare up at him.

"What did you expect?"

"I–" Everything I've done seems pithy. Stupid. "It doesn't matter."

He freezes, his hand resting at the top of my thigh. Rough fingers are mere breaths away from touching me and despite my words, *I ache.* If I arch my back his hand would be on me and he'll know how much my body desires exactly what he wants. My head screams at me as I fight even though I don't know why. Some deep seated need to provide *more* maybe? To be *more* than just sex as payment for a job?

But that's what we agreed to, and I know that.

I do know that.

"It's nothing," I repeat, sliding my hand down the front of his Henley. It's damp. I press the top patch but he doesn't wince, just watches me. Those eyes are unfathomable in the light that refuses to catch his face. I pull my hand away. Darkness covers it. I don't need to sniff it to know the tang that covers my skin. "Yours or his?" I whisper.

"His," Gabriel murmurs. His hand presses between my legs. A hiss elicits between his teeth. "Fuck, sweetness. I thought—"

I arch beneath him, letting him pin my arm over my head. "I don't want to want you this much," I whisper.

He laughs as two thick fingers slide into me easily. "It's not fair, is it?" he agrees, and groans. "Christ, you're tight *and* wet. Fucking perfection, sweetness. You know you're staying, don't you?"

I nod on a sob, already falling apart beneath him. "I need to be more than just sex for a job, Gabriel," I manage to force the words out.

Let me beg.

Please lie to me.

Say all the things I need to hear.

His fingers still inside me. "Make yourself come, Elena."

"What?" My preorgasmic haze shatters as I peer up at him. Salty drops coat my cheeks.

I wiggle my hips, but he refuses to move. The thick intrusion inside me leaves me aching but just being there isn't anywhere near enough for me to come.

"Give me your first orgasm. You're soaked. You're wearing my shirt. I want you to be mine." He nuzzles along my jawline, discovering tender spots I don't know I have. "Work yourself up on me and show me how you get yourself off."

"I—" Heat suffuses my face as I shut down internally even as a rush of fluid coats the insides of my thighs.

Gabriel uses his knees to press my thighs wide, preventing me from shutting my legs when I tense. "Come on, sweetness. Every time you fight me, I'll add an extra finger. How much can you stretch this pretty pussy for me?"

He slides a third inside me. I cry out at the burning pain that eases almost immediately. He pumps his hand once, coating his fingers and stops. The pleasure building instantly hits edging point and stays there.

I moan my frustration as he stares down at me, unmoving. "Please," I beg. "I need..."

"I know," Gabriel says softly. "I know, sweetness. I did something for you. Now I need something back. Can you do that for me? Show me," he coos, circling my throat with his other hand and trapping my air gently.

Everything so, so gently.

I gush for him. "Fuck," I whimper, rocking in time to the flex in his hand on my throat, syncing my movements with how he pulses and lets me breathe only to take my air away again.

"That's it. Good girl," he approves, timing my

rocks with his hand. "Keep going. I wanna see you cream on my hand tonight. Work that pretty little cunt on my fingers like they're your new favorite toy."

I whimper, straining to press past the second knuckles. Pressure builds and I push a hand between us, working my clit. Gabriel allows it, though the trade off is that he takes more of my air with each pulse.

My moans fill the treehouse, cut off each time I raise my hips, seeking greater friction.

"Stunning," he whispers as I lurch upright, pushing against his hand around my throat on a cry no one else hears and as I gush all over his hand.

"Gabriel—" I stutter out. My thighs strain, attempting to close as I force my pussy over the knuckles of all his fingers, impaling myself deeper on him.

"Christ, that's a beautiful sight." He leans down and licks my lips, sliding his tongue inside my mouth when I open for him.

Our mouths barely meet as he glides his tongue against mine. Pleasure ignites in me again. He spreads his fingers inside me and I cry out into his mouth. Dark eyes watch me, assessing my limits. The hand on my throat closes and doesn't let go. Breath escapes me. I can't inhale, but I keep trying, flailing in his hold as he murmurs his approval. His thumb works my clit fast, hand pumping inside me hard and rough. Faster than I can ever work myself.

I scream silently, already coming undone for him. Heat builds and builds as my orgasm crests but he doesn't release me. I come on his hand a second time, bucking my hips upward as he drives his hand deeper inside me than before. My scream tears at my throat, flexing beneath his hand.

"Need you," I mouth before he kisses me, his tongue tracing along mine sensually.

My shudders and shivers subside as he lets my breath flow back in, stroking my clit gently.

"Gabriel," I moan, rocking my hips. "I can't keep up with you."

He laughs softly. "Honey, when I'm here you'll have my dick in you so often that you'll beg me to leave."

"Never."

"I haven't fucked you yet." He catches my hand and drags it to the front of his pants, rubbing my palm over his hard length. "If you want to take me, I'll need to stretch this pretty pussy out a little more."

He over fills my hand.

"Fuck," I whisper finding the size of him.

Gabriel's fingers flex inside me. "Lie back, beautiful. Let me lick you."

I whimper as he pushes his shirt up over my breasts, exposing the scars on my skin. I cover them up but he knocks my hands away with a growl.

"Never hide from me, Elena. *Never*."

I nod as he pushes me back, completely bared to him, and let him spread me wide. His hands glide over my curves, his tongue tracing a similar path. Fluids that weren't mine are on my skin, his sheets.

"Get this off." I tug at his wet shirt. "I want to feel you warm against me."

"Let me turn up the furnace." The pressure between my legs disappears.

I let out a feral moan, still splayed out across his bed. Gabriel disappears for a moment then he's back. He strokes between my legs, his mouth hot and wet on my breasts.

"Gabriel—"

"Gabe." He raises his mouth to find mine. "Just Gabe, sweetness."

"Gabe," I whisper, tangling my fingers in his hair and stroking them through. "So silky."

His touch returns between my legs. "I'm gonna spend hours stretching you out, Elena. After tonight the only man you'll take is me, do you understand?"

It's the same *understood?* that he gave me when he left to find Oliver.

He slides two fingers inside me as I nod. My pussy pulses.

"I understand, Gabe."

"Tell me what you understand."

"It means you won't let me leave."

He adds a third finger and pushes in hard. I cry out. "Try that again, sweetness."

"It means I stay here with you forever."

He thrusts gently, working me smoother. Pressure builds quickly. I moan, lift my hips in time to his thrusts.

"Good girl. What else?"

"It means you've taken payment for what I needed."

A fourth finger. Hard shove. Harder thrust.

"Fuck." I bite my lip and look up at him with pleading eyes.

"Fix. It." His tone is as hard as his movements as he pushes his hand back into me.

I think fast, which isn't easy because even with his roughness, the feel of him working my body drags me closer and closer to orgasm. "You've done what I asked and I'm your reward. And I'm..." I don't know how to say the last part and look to him for help.

Gabe stares down at me, his hard face relentless as his touch gentles, four fingers gliding into me, out again. Fuck, I'm wet. I've never needed a man so much in my life. I want him so much it hurts. He holds my orgasm hostage with slow gentle touches when I know just how brutal he can be.

"You earn a reward every time you're good for me, sweetness. I'll show you how," he promises me. "What else?"

I gaze back at him, panicking. My body tightens as he cradles me close. "I don't know—"

"You can do this. Breathe, beautiful."

I nod, rocking my hips as he doesn't punish me this time. A fifth digit prods at my entrance. His thumb works its way into me, aided by the copious slick that soaks his bed.

"You'll stretch me to the point that I'm useless to another man and only yours," I whisper, choking on my own need.

"You're mine now," he murmurs, working his hand against me.

Knuckles bump my entrance. I groan at the tight, full, impossible feeling. "It won't fit," I gasp, clawing at his shoulder.

"We won't rush this," Gabe promises me. "I'll work you all night, gorgeous. Then I'm going to sink my cock into your stretched pussy after I've been arm deep in you for hours, and play with your nipples. You're going to soak my cock in your cum, over and over, and I'm not even going to fuck you. You're going to get used to the feeling of me inside you, sweetness, I promise. You'll learn to love my cock inside you so much that you'll feel empty without me."

His words are my poison. I shudder as his knuckles slip, one at a time inside me. It's a train wreck as I come for him, bearing down when I shouldn't, opening my mouth for his tongue as he invades every sacred place in me. I come as he glides his fist inside me and opens his hand.

"Fuck," I pant, shivering. *"Fuck, fuck—"*

My pussy grips his arm, fluttering as he groans. Gabe reaches down and grips his cock, arching over me. A few hard jerks and he spills his seed all over me, painting my belly and my scars and my breasts in white ropes as he shouts my name.

I moan at the depravity of it, my ruined pussy stretched out on his hand, him cumming all over my body.

"Fuck, you're the most beautiful creature I've ever seen, Elena. And you're mine," he whispers reverently.

I whimper as he slides his hand from my body and drives it back in again. My head tosses back, and I swear I lose sense of the world as the cycle restarts.

Our bodies press together, his mouth on mine in hungry, liquid kisses. Fluids smear across our skin as he works my body as he promised, letting me get used to the feel of him, his growing hardness trapped between us.

As the sun rises, he rolls me over to face the open forest, tucking the quilts over our bodies. The air has a deep chill to it. The furnace isn't quite keeping up.

"With me, sweetness." Gabe slides an arm under my head as I nearly pass out on him, barely able to arrange my body the way he asks.

He tucks my hips, lifting one leg as he slides

behind me. I close my eyes, exhausted and barely conscious as he kisses and sucks at the skin on my neck.

"Deep breath, beautiful," he murmurs, playing with my clit. "Can you come for me once more?"

"Are you kidding?" My eyes drop shut. "You've worn me out, Gabe."

"I hope not," he rasps as he jerks his hips and fills me with that log of cock between his legs. "Now we really start."

CHAPTER SIX

ELENA

*M*y scream rips from me as Gabe angles my head back and seals his mouth over mine, stealing the sound for himself. A deep groan reverberates within his chest as he sinks balls deep inside me and settles there.

"Fuck, that's good, sweetness," he murmurs his appreciation against my lips, dropping his hand to my hips and pinning me in place. "Now, be perfect and don't move, no matter what. I want to enjoy the feeling of the cunt that belongs to the wife of the man I just killed soaking my cock for the next hour while you come for me. Just for me, sweetness. Understood?"

I jerk, trying to breathe. The stretch of him is like

nothing I've ever experienced before. My lungs refuse to fill with air. Gabe laughs softly in my ear as he reaches around me. One hand finds a nipple to play with, the other toys with my clit.

"Will an orgasm help take the edge off, Elena? Just a little?" He strums me as I writhe, and he clucks. His arms fold around me like a vice. "None of that. You stay nice and still. I'm not going to fuck you and you're not going to ride me. Is that clear?" His voice hardens, bringing me back a fraction.

I nod frantically, winding my legs around his where he propped me before.

"Better," he approves. "Now, relax and let your body take over. Be my little toy for the next hour, sweetness. You're all mine now."

I moan as the first tendrils of my orgasm reach for me. I soak in gentle touch, sweet and tender. Like he cares. Like he—

I bite back a sob but it catches me out and finds its release anyway.

"Shhh, sweetness. It's okay. It's alright," Gabe coos in my ear. "Shatter for me. Break apart. It's what you need."

I sob again as my orgasm slams into me from nowhere. My body bears down, taking the thickness of him impossibly deep inside.

"Fuck," Gabe swears. "Hell, woman. Tighten that little pussy like that around me again and I'll soak your insides too fast."

I mumble my reply into his shoulder, my head turned into his arm. He nuzzles into my neck, pressing tender kisses against my throat as his fingers toy my nipples, squeezing and plucking rhythmically.

The pressure I just got rid of rebuilds almost instantly. I hate my body for its attempt at tenacity when I thought it was exhausted. The next orgasm hits me as I squeeze my legs together. Gabe tuts and taps my ankles apart, enjoying himself far too much.

"Is this your reward or my punishment?" I mutter. "I can't believe I cooked for you."

He strokes my nipples gently. "Did you say you cooked, sweetness?" he murmurs thoughtfully.

"Yeah." I snort and moan in the same breath. Not impossible and, I think, quite talented. "I had this stupid idea of you coming h– back, and me feeding you to say thank you. But instead you carved my body up like it was your personal table to eat at, and– *shit!*" I shriek as he rolls us, pinning me onto my back with my hands over my head beneath one of his, his cock still lodged deep inside me.

"You cooked for me." Gabe's forehead rests gently on mine. "After what I did for you?"

"I–yes?" I admit. "It's stupid. I said that. Let me up," I beg as tears cloud my vision.

I hate that he can see me like this as the sun crests the horizon, breaking through the haze that has concealed all the truths I hid from myself last night.

I sold myself to this man to prevent another man from killing me.

I gave away the last things about myself that I loved and he will never know or care.

And in that time I convinced myself that I matter to him. That I care about him too.

The truth is that I know nothing about this man and he knows nothing about me, either. All we know about each other is limited to a brief negotiation and last night's marathon round of sex.

My tears fall unhindered as he watches me. I hate myself all the more.

For years I managed not to show any emotion to Oliver. I never let him see me cry. Now, in front of this man I barely know? Here I am, letting everything out. He does me one favour, one thing, and I sell him my dignity along with my soul.

Or my heart.

Oh hell.

I haven't. I can't have.

Or maybe I did.

Gabriel Decker appears to have come to the same conclusion as me at the same time.

"Sweetness," he murmurs in a hushed voice. The thickness lodged inside me swells.

I cry out, an involuntary sound I can't prevent as he breaks his promise and begins to move.

I should hurt. Everything should ache and burn and tear.

It doesn't.

Gabe cradles me in his arms like I'm the most precious thing he's ever seen. He holds me close as I struggle for him, my legs tucked near his hips. I cry out when he reaches down and lifts one of my legs over his shoulders, rearing over me.

"Hold on," he murmurs. "You can't hurt me."

But I can hurt you.

I hear what he doesn't say, gripping his arms tight as he slams deep into me. My head tosses back, and a darkness that I swear the sun already chased away filters across my vision. My cries are distant as he moves over me, his words faint, though his touch is warm and close.

At no point does he leave me and I know he's always there. Even when my throat turns raw and I can't hear him anymore, I know his arms are wrapped around me, cradling me to his chest.

His mouth seals to mine as I fade, his hips jerking as he fills me, hot and thick to the brim.

Gabe whispers words I know he shouldn't even as my mind refuses to recognize them.

And I think I say them back.

GABE'S BATH is as warm and comfy in the sunlight as it was in the starlight. He has a collection of scented oils that I doubt are for him, and his tub is oversized to fit him which means I fit there too.

His arms wrap around me as he pours oil through my hair and combs it out. "Merry Christmas, sweetness."

"Merry... it is?" I count the days in my head. "Oh, my God. It is."

He shushes me when I try to sit up, counting my days out a second time. The head massage he offers drops me back into a semi-awake state, and he resumes combing my curls.

"How do you know what to do?" I ask drowsily.

The scented water soothes my body, the aches we've created, the way he's reformed me. It's not just physical. I've changed inside and out. I know that even if my mind struggles to accept that fact in such a short period of time.

"I didn't always live alone, Elena." Gabe pauses in his combing. "You're not the only one who tried to have a family."

I grip his thigh and twist. That creates a whole new world of aches as water sloshes around us but I ignore them. "Before?"

He seems to get what I'm not saying. "Yeah." He winds my curls through the rake comb and continues to tug it through my hair in the same gentle method he used before I interrupted his rhythm. "Before I was deployed that time, I had a partner. She was pregnant." his voice rasps.

"Gabe," I whisper.

"I didn't come home when we planned. Shit went sideways. My deployment was a lot longer than expected because my operation overseas turned into a war camp rescue that ended in my best friend and a whole lot of other men I loved dying. I brought him home. When I came back, she wasn't there." He shrugs, still combing my hair with steady hands. "She'd given up, moved on. Decided I wasn't coming back. My little girl is being raised by another man. I'm not allowed to see her based on my psych evaluation afterwards and a court who never met me in my absence."

"Jesus." I lean into him, pressing my body to his. I have no idea what I'm doing apart from offering up any spec of warmth that I possibly can. "That's— it's not fair," I whisper.

His mouth crooks into a smile, and his hands hold me without a single tremor. "I killed a man for a woman I met three days ago without a second's thought. Then I told you that you can never leave. Perhaps they were right, sweetness."

I stare at him. "I feel like I'm supposed to say something supportive. That you should be able to get your girl back."

He shrugs again. "One day, if she wants, maybe she can find me. But I'm not a safe man, Elena. You shouldn't be here." His face hardens as he pulls me closer to him. "You do know that, don't you?"

I lean into him. "I cooked for you."

He stills. "You said that before."

My heart beats faster. "When you were...away," I say carefully. "I cried. I screamed. I ranted and raved and kicked things. I don't think I broke anything apart from my sanity a few times. And I drank a lot of coffee," I admit. "It's good coffee."

"It is."

"And then I did what I do when I care about someone or I'm happy or comfortable. I cooked."

He watches me. "Were you happy and comfortable after screaming your heart out when I locked you in here, sweetness?"

I return his study. "Yes."

Gabe blinks.

"Up here, it's quiet. Beautiful. Peaceful. I could think. And when I can think, I create. So I did."

His mouth twitches beneath his beard. "I have a refrigerator full of meals, do I?"

I laugh at him. "Do I look like a girl who cooks meals, Mister Decker? You have three berry pies, a pudding, because I found a mix and I could—shush. Let me finish. A beehive cake, a strawberry gateau and a honey sponge cake. Oh, and a coffee roll but that's gone because I also comfort eat when I'm sad." I finish my list and offer him a happy smile.

He huffs at me and slides his huge hands over my curves, squeezing his fingers in until dimples appear in my skin. "Woman, if you're set on feeding me, I don't think I'll ever want to leave you here alone ever again."

I swear I glow.

"So does that mean we're okay?" I peek at him through my lashes.

"Fucking flirt," he growls, dropping the comb. His hand cups my nape and he pulls me hard into him.

I gasp as he seals our mouths together, his tongue teasing mine in liquid kisses before he twists me in the tub. Sloshing water everywhere, Gabe pulls my legs to either side of his and pushes me down.

His cock nudges my entrance as I widen my eyes at him.

"Oh, no, Gabe. No. There's no way. I can't—"

His growl against my mouth shuts me up as his hips surge upward. "If I want to fuck the woman I love, then I'll have her," he grates against my lips, then pulls back. "Unless I'm hurting you?"

I nearly laugh out loud. After everything that we've done in the last twelve hours, *hurt* doesn't even come close. But I know what he means. There's intentional pain and careless pain in sex. He's talking about the latter. Real damage, tearing me because we didn't prepare.

But the rest of his words catch up with my brain and I stop laughing.

The smile fades from his face.

"Sweetness?"

"You said that before. Last night. Didn't you?" My brain is soup, but I know what I heard. I mean, I think I did.

Gabe sweeps wayward curls back from my face that spring back into my peripheral vision anyway. "I didn't think you heard me," he says quietly. "You were pretty out of it by then."

"I was, but I remember…" I frown. "This is fast."

"It is," he acknowledges. "But what we are isn't normal, either." Gabe sighs, placing his hands on my hips and lifts me. His cock slides out of me.

I cry out at the sudden loss. "What are you doing?" I feel empty. Bereaved. "Gabe?"

He leans his head back against the edge of the tub and closes his eyes. One hand reaches over his head to a cabinet with a combination lock on it just within his reach. He spins a dial on it and pulls the small door open. A set of keys sit in his hand.

He opens his eyes, catches my hand and places the keys in them. "You know how I feel. For me, this is real. For you? This is yours. Your choice, Elena. Your freedom."

Gabe closes his eyes and tips his head back again.

I stare at the keys in my hand, what he just gave me.

My heart beats that much faster.

CHAPTER SEVEN

GABE

*E*lena doesn't move. She doesn't breathe. I expect her to stumble her way out of the tub, dress and run her ass out of my house and back down the mountain. All the way back to Hope Peak.

She does none of those things.

"Elena," I warn her. "If you don't move, that offer will expire. I'll take those damn keys back and you'll never leave this room again."

"Like a princess in a tower," she muses.

"What?" I can't help the abrupt tone that snaps out of me. She's absurd. So am I. This whole thing is a farce. It can't be real no matter what I say.

"You can't keep me, Gabe. I saw the combination." She's laughing at me.

It takes everything I have not to grab the keys from her hand and throw them off the damn ledge. "I'll change the fucking combination." *Or get a better safe.*

"You could do that."

I get the impression that she's enjoying this little power exchange too much. Hells, all I want to do is take her over my lap and spank her bare ass bright red. Maybe teach her a few different ways to use those holes of hers.

"I could, huh?" A new fantasy takes hold before I can shake it. One I fully intend to play with later.

Elena is still in the water but her body vibrates with coiled tension. She's seconds from bolting, and I'm seconds from crushing her back to me and revoking everything I just told her.

"You said once that if I ran, you'd chase me. That the punishment wouldn't be worth me leaving."

My cock stiffens painfully beneath us. "I said that, yeah." Every breath is ragged. I can't tell if they're mine or hers.

Elena leans forward and places her sweet lips against mine. The kiss is light and chaste and all the things neither of us need.

"This is me running," she whispers against my mouth.

Then she's out of the water and across the floor. The first key is in the lock before my brain has caught up with the action. She startles a laugh out of me as her feet patter into the stairwell.

This. Woman.

I give her a decent count before I haul my ass out of the tub, letting the water out. Hell, I even have time to dry and dress before she starts tackling the locks downstairs. My boots are on by then. Best yet? The snow I've been waiting on drifts across the forest, dusting the tops of the trees.

It'll be a hard, fast chase. She can have a head start.

So when the door opens at the bottom of my house, the harness is in my hand.

I step off the edge of the platform, her name on my lips. Seeing my woman flee into the forest, knowing she has minutes at best before I catch her, is the sexiest damn thing I've ever seen.

And if I have doubts?

My sweetness left the keys in the lock and headed away from the town, deeper into the mountains where there are no paths. Where she knows I'll find her anyway.

Fuck, I love her.

I loved her the moment she turned up on my doorstep begging for help, and nothing has changed since then. I wait a little longer before I head into the forest.

There's nothing better than hearing those little

sounds she makes when I surprise her. And I have every intention of earning as many of those sounds as I possibly can today.

Merry fucking Christmas to me.

EPILOGUE

GABE

*T*he table at Perfect Brews is free of Christmas decorations as I sit across from the man who served with me before all hell broke loose in a place I'll never return to in person but that haunts dreams I never talk about. Not even to Elena.

For Drake, he has his own battles to fight.

"Why did you send her to me?" I turn the wedding ring over in my hands. It's too big for her, but it's the right fit for me. Today is a quiet cere-mony. Drake will be there, and a friend of hers. She doesn't want anything big and I hate crowds.

A year after Elena turned up on my mountain, she's still with me. We decided to make it official, and her name is about to become Elena Decker. She never did get around to that paperwork, though there was some other to do after her ex passed due to a terrible incident with a mafia run in. At least, that was how the local papers reported his death.

Deboning seemed about right for the circumstances all around. Bloody, messy and personal.

Like I said, it fit.

Drake holds my gaze and shrugs. "She needed help, You seemed like the right man for the job." He nods to the wedding band in my hand. "Looks like it worked out."

"Yeah, you're a regular match maker." I lean back and pass the ring over to him. He's holding onto it until the ceremony. "I hear that you're not staying in town though."

Drake shrugs again. His go to. "Sitting around wasn't doing me any favors. I picked up some work. I thought I might try a change of scenery."

Hope Peak is pretty, and safe. I nod. "Whatever you need. Are you going back to engineering?"

He snorts. "Like I said, change of scene. Trying my hand at security work."

I raise my eyebrows. "You're becoming a doorman at a club?" I doubt that will work out. He has the patience of an ant with the brains of the smartest man in the room.

"Hell, no. Body guarding. At a ranch. I think." He scratches scruff on his chin.

"That's...unique."

"Almost as good as what you do."

I nod. "Almost."

"Time's up, boys."

I spin in my seat to find Elena standing behind me in a pale blue dress she bought at a second hand shop in town. She didn't care for a white or cream dress or any other marriage tradition, having already been there once. What she did care about was the cake and I've been eating the trial stuff for weeks.

There's a huge one, enough to feed a small army, in the back of the Perfect Brew's cold room. I reckon we'll leave the damn thing here. Thankfully she made it in town at Drake's place.

"You look beautiful," I murmur, taking in the dress that sweeps to her ankles from a scalloped neckline. Tiny flowers adorn the soft blue lace all over. Her hair is caught up in a knot at her nape. A few flyaway curls have escaped. "Perfect."

"Thank you. You brush up well." She touches my trimmed beard.

I went to a barber this morning, avoiding eye contact with the mirror for as long as possible. Eventually I had to look and found...

A man I don't hate as much as I expected to on the other side.

Apparently we're both on a healing path together. All the sappy shit wrapped up with a strawberry blonde bombshell and cake.

So much fucking cake.

I love her though and she loves me back to my shock. That's what matters.

"Better get going." Drake rises, holding onto the rings. "The church isn't going anywhere but I think there's another wedding booked after us."

"Alright. Sweetness?"

Elena rises onto her toes and presses a kiss on the cheek I present to her. "I like this. But I love my wild man better."

"I can do wild, sweet thing."

I hold her hand and let her lead me to the small church on the edge of town she's chosen for our vows.

It could be anywhere. That wouldn't matter to me. What matters is her in the same room as me, and her agreeing to whatever she needs most.

Hell, I can't believe I'm lucky enough to have found her. The woman I fell in love with at first sight who loves me back.

Utter perfection.

THANK YOU FOR READING

Thank you for reading *Mountain Man's Love at Frost Sight.* Please leave a review. Drake's story is coming in **Her Mountain Man Bodyguard** available in 2026.

ABOUT THE AUTHOR

USA Today Bestselling author Sofia Aves writes fast-paced police romances, sizzling military units, steamy cowboys with a Montana backdrop and the occasional cheeky god. Sofia writes kidlit for charity and has over one hundred and fifty publications across six not-so-super-secret pen names. As acquisitions editor for Evernight and Evernight Teen publishing she loves discovering new talent in romance and YA spaces, and is a mum of three crazies in a returned veteran household. Sofia has two overly large fur babies who think they're teacup puppies, a duck who prefers to eat from a dog bowl and two axolotls named after a dragon and a firebird.

Sofia lives near Brisbane, Australia, where she has her own alpaca park, Lorendel.

www.sofiaaves.com

Sign up to <u>Sofia's newsletter</u> and get a free Blue Blooded Brothers book.

Haven't read the Z Boy's prequel? Get it for free here:
A TABLE FOR TEN
Follow Sofia on
BookBub
Twitter
Instagram
<u>Facebook</u>

READ SOFIA'S SERIES

Blue Blooded Brothers
Collision
Politics & Paperwork
Blindsided
Sentinel
Mugshots & Candy Canes
Impact
Reckoning
Red Hart Ranch
Snow on the Range
Siren on the Range
Sundown on the Range
Spirit on the Range
Ash on the Range
Mistletoe on the Range (2025)
Forgotten Mountain Man
Texan Devils

Ranger's Wish
Ranger Bedevilled
Ranger's Passion
Ranger's Fury
Ranger's Wrath
Ranger's Storm
Snapdragons & Seductions
Summer with a Ranger
Merry with a Ranger
Beach Duty Collection
Playing to Win
Off Boarding
Vicious Slash
Zero Pointer
Off Stage Fling
Rippton Allstars
Crushing It
Glacial Force
Rippton Creatives
Study Games
Make Me, Break Me
Twisted Obsession
Spring Break with a Mafia Prince
A Royally Fake French Menage
Angel Shot
Jericho Chimeras
Puck Me Always
Puck My Heart
Puck me Sideways

Z Boys
King
Joker
Hearts
Ace
Mayhem & Mistletoe
Ruski
Fast Track to Love
Speed Trap
Klauss Brothers
Zander
Keegan
Gallo Empire *with Jade Marshall*
Splintered Vows
Fractured Vows
Fierce Vows
Savage Covenant

Rom Coms
She's A Hot Christmas Mess
Boats, Moats and Root Beer Floats

Writing Romantasy as
SOFIA SHELLEY
Dead Poets Sorority

· · ·

WRITING Reverse Harem Dark Romance as
DOVE PRIEST
Recurve Ridge

KIDLIT WRITING as
JO SEYSENER
The OCD Elf
The OCD Elf's Great Reindeer Calamity
Greg and the Egg

WRITING YA as
JOSS PHOENIX
Alchem Academy
HIDE FROM US

WRITING spicy paranormal romance as
RAVEN HUSH
Club Fray
Darkest Desires
Purge
Kidnapped By Claws
Ruin
Shadow Lords
Sinner's End
Heaven's Gate (2026)
Monster Brides

Phoenix's Eternal Flame
Kraken's Vow
Krampus' Christmas Bride
Silent Sentinels Duet
Reflections of Silence
Echoes in the Void
Monsters In New York
Feral Moon Rising
Dark Water Refuge

www.ingramcontent.com/pod-product-compliance
Lightning Source LLC
Chambersburg PA
CBHW032109170626
46808CB00008B/2994